Hunted

Hunted
The Lone Wolf Hunter

A Modern Day Robin Hood Retelling

KC Freeman

FIRST EDITION: MARCH 2022

Dedication

To my loving husband who always gives me fresh inspiration for fun, romantic stories.

Chapter 1

Hand trembling as the mouse hovered over the "Confirm" button, Rob's mind raced with doubts. Would he be caught? What kind of jail sentence would he get for stealing money from a big-wig politician's phony charity and redistributing the wealth to those more deserving? How about leaking the senator's dirty scams with full cooperation from the largest and most successful government contractor, Nottingham, Inc.? He seriously doubted he'd be granted whistleblower protection.

Caught? Nah! Impossible. He was the best at his job, hacking his way through every top-notch security website around the globe. Albeit, mostly with pure intentions. He was an "ethical" hacker after all. An extremely well-paid one, too. There wasn't a classified program anywhere he couldn't break into without a trace. That was why the Federal government contractor he worked for had him on lockdown most days with his own private building and his own private office. They even chipped in for a company car when he'd pushed back at his last contract extension. Rob hadn't bothered to tell them that he didn't drive cars – motorcycles, yes – cars, no. His contract even paid for the car to remain parked in a secured lot with 24/7 surveillance.

Suckers!

So, why the need to steal from one of the main persons responsible for his nice, hefty contract?

Because Rob just couldn't let the sons-of-bitches get away with siphoning money appropriated by the government for needy families for a senator's own less-charitable pet projects? Real people were in dire need and that asshole was living the high life on the money meant to ease their sufferings.

No, he wasn't that noble.

This started as simple revenge. It was the sole reason he took the job at Nottingham. Bring down the company, and all its accomplices, seemed a fitting retribution for the extinction of his entire family.

But nothing is ever simple, especially when it comes to revenge.

Rob hadn't even known about the senator's involvement, or his current underhanded schemes. He'd discovered the senator's shenanigans by accident while tracing a string of financial transactions from the source (United States Treasury) through the Senate appropriations process to the final recipient. When the funds didn't appear where they should have been, he hacked a few dark sites to discover what became of the monies. He'd suspected the system had been hacked by a foreign entity. That was usually the case. But the more he followed the breadcrumbs, the clearer it became. All trails led straight back to Senator Johnson's personal overseas accounts. The IRS would never have been able to follow this audit trail, but no information system was too complex for Rob Holden.

Knowing his own boss was neck-deep in the corruption sealed his decision. The money had been appropriated for a contract with Nottingham to help in refugee resettlements in the Middle East. Instead, half of the funds ended up the senator's accounts. Less than 10% had gone towards the actual work mandate.

As Rob saw it, stealing from the sleazy crooked elite and giving to those truly in need would serve society the best. With a little sleight of hand, and just like a magician, the funds from the latest transfer to the senator were re-routed to another organization working on the same relief efforts.

Okay, for a second he'd contemplated keeping the money for himself, but he wasn't that type of guy. Besides, he was an *ethical* hacker, he had a personal set of standards and stealing for himself wasn't in his DNA.

What better than a little bit of revenge for his family, as well as for the downtrodden refugees? Pretty soon, the cops would catch on, or at least the media would with all the classified information he was leaking to dark websites. But the odds of them tracing anything back to him was next to zero.

Still, the blinking message on his computer screen blared like neon lights in his eyes. *Please Confirm Your Transaction.*

Yes, confirm you, *Mister Big Ass Untouchable Sanctimonious Senator,* wish to divert millions in funds from your personal account to a real charity.

Taking a deep breath, Rob's middle finger twitched a split second before decisively snapping down on the right-click button.

Transaction Confirmed.

3:14 AM IN LARGE EYE-shattering digital flashed. Adeline squinted as her hand slapped around to turn off her damn phone vibrating against the glass nightstand to the tune of "The Imperial March".

Who the fuck calls at this time of day? Her fingers connected with the slim cell. For a second, an image of flinging the phone across the room flared in the back of her mind.

"What?" she barked.

"Good morning, sunshine. Didn't wake you, did I?" The gravelly, yet cheerful, voice on the other end of the line sent waves of irritation through her veins. Vincent, her so-called partner. Why the Agency top brass insisted on burdening her with yet another overly eager, certain to crash and burn, partner was beyond her comprehension. She'd just run him off like the last dozen or so. Besides, there was something creepy about him. Adeline hadn't put her finger on why he gave her the willies, but her instincts were always on target.

"If the sun ain't up, it ain't morning. What do you want, Vinny?"

"Well, crime doesn't stop for your beauty sleep. Besides I thought you preferred nights anyway." The sound of him clearing his throat rattled over the speaker. "And, please, for pity's sake... stop calling me Vinny. You know I hate that."

Her lips curled up on one side. "Why?"

Silence.

Adeline flipped on the bedside lamp and sat up. No more sleep in her immediate future. Might as well deal with what crap the Agency wanted her to check out. "Fine. Fill me in. What are we looking at?"

After a short, relieved sigh, Vincent gave her the scoop. High-ranking politician had his personal finances breached less than an hour ago. Lots of money vanished from his overseas accounts into thin air. And to top it off, the news outlets were already plugging an announcement for the scandal of the year from an anonymous source.

She ended the call with "… Meet you in ten." One leg already in her navy linen slacks and one arm clipping her lacey bra clasp together, Adeline stumbled over to the bathroom. Icy water splashed on her face threw off the remnants of sleep. Brushing her naturally pearly white teeth, Adeline went through her head all the known criminal hackers in the agency's database. She'd memorized them all from a case a couple of months back when the Federal Reserve security had been breached. Of course, it'd turned out to be a group of teenagers working out of a garage in Toronto. Big smack in the face for the information security team overseeing the Fed.

Pulling her mane of platinum, almost silver, hair into a tight ponytail, Adeline grinned at the image in the mirror. Tracking down bad guys was like hunting, which was her favorite activity. At least this way, no one usually ended up all bloody. Well, not all the time anyway.

Vincent's words rang in her ears. "The locals are calling the culprit *The Lone Wolf.* He or she has been leaking classified intelligence here and there over the last five years, but apparently this time it's super big. Got the entire government complex in an uproar. This isn't the first time he's stolen money from DC bigwigs either, but he's been too wily to catch."

A wily wolf? Intriguing. Of course, they couldn't catch him.

It takes a wolf to catch one.

OVER FIVE HUNDRED EMPLOYEES at Nottingham, Inc. and not one fit the profile for an expert hacker pilfering money and information. Sixteen hours after being so rudely awakened from her smoking and thoroughly wet dream involving a Finnish natural hot spring and a mix-match of FIFA international stars, Adeline was no closer to catching *The Lone Wolf* than before she arrived at the company's headquarters fifteen hours ago. Being unable to fulfill her primal, carnal needs over the last few months had her frustrated and left every nerve raw. She was tired, hungry, and more than a smidge cranky.

If Vincent offered one more time to get her a Snickers bar from the vending machine, she would not be responsible for the resulting black eye she'd give him.

Rubbing the bridge of her nose did scant to relieve the pressure building behind her eyes. "Mrs. Pelham, are you absolutely certain these," her hand waved over the desk cluttered with manila folders, "are all Nottingham's employees? No more independent contractors? No summer interns? Hourly wage night janitor? No one else?" At this point, the one thing Adeline knew was that the hacker was not in the stack of files.

The pale-faced waif with shoulder-length blonde wavy hair, perfectly applied cosmetics, and the brightest shade of red lipstick and nail polish Adeline ever witnessed, stared past her. Despite the enormous rock on her left-hand ring finger, the ditz seemed rather enamored with her partner, Vincent, and reserved all her one-word answers for him.

Seriously? She was the lead agent on this case, not the baby-faced man in the gray striped Armani suit behind here.

Even if he did somewhat resemble Leonardo DiCaprio, the incompetent admin assistant should be responding to her.

After another annoyed sigh, Adeline turned to glare at her partner. "You wrap this up." Her stilettos clicking loudly on the dated, multi-colored speckled tile, she marched down the hall and out the main building only to be met by the roar of airplanes piercing her delicate eardrums. "Ugh." Why did federal government contractors, appropriately known as Beltway Bandits, establish their headquarters at the damn airport? They made butt-loads of money. Why not more prestigious digs in the middle of the action on 14th Street in DC?

The city is no place for wolves.

Might explain why she was the real lone wolf.

A deep-buried need coiled in her chest. The need to hunt. And not just for some white-collared criminal. No, it had been ages since she'd allowed herself to give in to her primal needs. Perhaps that was why she was so cranky lately. She'd ignored her true nature for too long, but racing along the forest floor by herself, without a pack...it only made her more aware of her loneliness.

Flinging a leg over her classic 1978 Harley-Davidson Super Glide – best twenty grand she'd ever spent – Adeline let the stress ooze out her pores, releasing the muscle tension in her shoulders. The hacker would still be there tomorrow. Let Vincent handle the administrative crap that came with this job. A pinch of guilt rose up. She wasn't one to let her duties slide, especially not for personal reasons. But she needed to clear her head in order to sniff out the criminals. In her present state, she'd probably look the hacker square in the face and not realize it was him or her.

Now, it was time to hunt. The only hunting permissible within the city limits, where the prey were more of the six foot plus and bulging muscles variety.

Twenty minutes later, Adeline pulled up to her hotel, parking in the secured lot underneath the ancient colonial building in Old Town Alexandria. The ride had cleared her head, but the rest of her body was primed, aching for release. The animal in her needed more than the mundane human world allowed, but she was forced to live by their rules now. So instead of aiming her bike out to the rural mountains bordering West Virginia and Maryland where she could've run free, she'd turned back to the urban equivalent of the hunt... a local bar, and well renowned "meat market" along the waterfront.

Oh, how civilized I've become.

Instead of running free in the wilderness and hunting to quench her blood lust, she'd evolved to tracking a different type of prey in the urban jungle. Over time, Adeline adapted by pushing down her inner beast's need to kill and replaced it with more carnal desires. Sex took the edge off her more basic needs.

Adeline pushed the morose thought aside as she entered the already darkened pub. Just past happy hour, the place was packed solid with the professional government class of patrons. All in their nice suits with ties askew, dropping names and trying to one up each other on who had a better gig on Capitol Hill.

Why did she keep coming back to this bar anyway? The scenery rarely changed. Oh yeah, easy prey.

Her eyes scanned the bar, looking for anyone with a glimmer of something special, something to excite her inner beast, something to satisfy the craving deep within, the throbbing ache in need of release.

Bingo!

In the far corner, away from the hordes of twenty and thirty-somethings looking for a hookup, engrossed in his laptop screen with a half empty pilsner and untouched bacon cheeseburger and fries, was the perfect quarry.

Dark gold curls had a halo effect around a rugged, masculine face. Little more than a five o'clock shadow caused Adeline's fingers to twitch imagining the stinging burn of the stubble against her own smooth ivory skin. Eyes were shielded by wire-rimmed glasses, hid the most important aspect of the human face. He wasn't dressed like the rest. Instead, a worn gray t-shirt with 'West Point' faded almost into the thin cotton, highlighted statue-worthy pectorals and showcased bulging biceps that strained the material. Most importantly, he was alone.

A quick stop at the bar, Adeline didn't even need to place her order. Kathy, the lanky bartender who worked every night to support herself and her good-for-nothing boyfriend, had her usual scotch and amaretto poured ready. "Thanks. Put it on my tab. And keep them coming... over there." Her head tilted towards the far end of the bar.

Kathy winked, her soft, melodic voice resonated in Adeline's head, "Gotcha. Happy hunting."

The bartender knew Adeline's deep, dark secret. Well, she'd recognized like kind when she'd first stepped into the place months ago. The bartender was the only other wolf shifter still in the Mid-Atlantic States. What held the bartender here without a pack, Adeline hadn't bothered to ask.

She often wondered why she didn't escape the urban sprawl for wilder fields, find other wolf shifters. Kathy had once told her of large packs roaming the Northwest – Montana, Wyoming, and Idaho. The idea of heading west in search of a pack had tempted Adeline for about half a minute. The truth was she thrived on the action. Yeah, she was lonely, but her spirit needed the adrenaline rush her job provided. And her inherent talents made her damn good at it.

The floor was sticky with spilled alcohol. She hated to think what the tips of her stilettos would look like at the end of the night. Adeline sidestepped an intoxicated, overly confident barrel-chested man eyeing her like a piece of candy. A grimy hand reached out and grabbed her upper arm. Turning to face her assailant, she allowed her eyes to transform to their wolf-state. No words were spoken, but the man beat a hasty retreat away from her and out the door. By the spooked look that crossed his face, he wouldn't be back anytime soon, if ever.

Kathy's giggle floated through Adeline's mind. "Don't scare off the clientele, please," followed by another giggle.

Just a few more steps ... the sexy man was still engrossed in his computer screen. Hadn't even looked up to see her coming straight towards him. *Geez, hope he's not watching porn on that thing.*

"Excuse me. Mind if I join you?" She kept her voice soft but had to boost the volume over the crowd noise.

He jumped as if shocked by a live wire.

"Sorry, didn't mean to startle you." Maybe this was a bad idea. Although smoking hot, he seemed a little jittery, like a rabbit after getting the first sniff of a predator nearby.

"No. No. That's fine. Just wasn't expecting anyone." He straightened up, side-eyed his laptop before slamming the lid closed. "Please." He waved for her to sit across from him. "Can I get the waitress …"

"No. I have everything I need." Adeline raised her glass, the amber liquid shimmering in the glare of a jumbo television behind the man's head. Thankfully, the bar kept the screens off news channels. The white-collared crowd got enough politics during the day at work. No one wanted to listen to that garbage off the clock, especially Adeline.

Nodding, he smiled as she slid across the bench. "I see." His eyes darted around, and his mouth opened to speak again, but abruptly closed.

Adeline stretched her hand across the table. "Hi, I'm Adeline Marion. You are?"

A strong hand grasped her own, as his other hand reached up and removed his glasses. Beautiful hazel eyes with specks of green gazed at her from under lush golden lashes. "Robin Holden. Nice to meet you, Adeline." The way her name rolled off his tongue, past his full lips sent a pulsating vibration through her limbs, radiating down to her core.

"Well, Robin," she breathed, "what shall we do?" Their hands were still entwined.

His right eyebrow arched, almost disappearing under his shaggy hair. "Oh, I can think of a few things."

Chapter 2

Rob kicked in the door to his studio apartment. Thankfully, he lived within walking distance to his favorite pub on the waterfront, and to the Metro for transportation to and from work while his company car sat idle. No amount of alcohol could justify the dream he was having. If it was the alcohol, he wanted more of it, on a daily basis because the vision swimming before his eyes was breathtaking.

But she couldn't be a dream. The feel of her smooth skin underneath his palms and the urgent crush of her lush lips on his neck... no, she had to be real.

Was this stunning woman with the glacial silver hair and matching metallic eyes really into him? Was that even possible?

They talked until the bartender had kicked them out. He hadn't even noticed that they were the only patrons left in the place. Actually, he hadn't noticed anyone or anything else all night.

The way Adeline's eyes had roved over him like he was a banquet for the starving lit a fire within him that he hadn't known existed. Every fiber of his being strummed in tune with the movements of her mouth as she spoke. For the life of him, he couldn't remember a word she said. However, every expression that crossed her beautiful face he knew by heart. Like the way her nose crinkled with disgust when a drunken man had slammed into their table, apparently on his way to the bathroom in the back. He'd laughed with delight as her entire face transformed from sexy vixen to that of an annoyed child. The way her eyelashes fanned out to frame her eyes, thick and lush casting a shadow over her cheeks when she blinked – he would've sworn his heart had leapt out of his chest every time she peered up at him through those lashes. Every smile sent shivers through his body, sending goosebumps across his flesh.

When they'd been kicked out, she'd taken his hand and somehow here they were at his place and her hands were diving underneath his shirt, running all over his chest and abs, then one hand strayed down ...

Oh. My. God.

A shudder ran through his entire body. The door banged shut behind him and suddenly he was thrown against it, luscious lips devoured his own. They'd barely made it the three blocks from the pub and had made a temporary pit stop in an alley on the way as a cop car passed, considering their indecent appearance. Somewhere along the way, the top button of his faded jeans had popped off and Adeline's blouse had come completely unbuttoned.

Oh, he couldn't think straight with her anywhere near him, much less stroking her fingers all over his body that way. He was close to bursting as it was already. Gently, Rob pushed her away. "Hey, hold on." The most unusual set of eyes stared back at him as she panted heavily against his own mouth. "No need to rush." Her head cocked to the side and her eyes narrowed slightly. A wicked, lopsided grin quirked up one side of her swollen lips, now completely devoid of lipstick.

"Slow?" Her fingers spread the front of his jeans apart, the zipper ripping downward. The tips caressed up and down over his briefs, his cock straining for freedom. "Whatever you say." Without warning, she knelt in front of him, her hands shrugging down his jeans on each side of his hips until the material pooled at his ankles. Looking up at him from under the darkest, thickest ebony lashes he'd ever seen, a truly wicked smile grew revealing perfect white teeth. Her tongue darted out and ran along her pouty lower lip.

Holy smokes! This woman could make me cum with a simple look.

Warm, smooth hands reached behind him, slipping by the hem of his briefs to cup his ass. Her sharp nails scratched down his buttocks, leaving a slight burning trail, before hooking into the fabric. A soft ripping noise followed as she yanked the garment off his body and casually tossed it away.

This must be a dream.

Dream or no, the sudden warmth that trickled up and down his cock as her tongue treated him like a lollipop evoked a loud moan from deep within his chest. The back of his head thudded against the door behind him as his knees went weak. After enduring the candy treatment for just about as much as he could bear, she suddenly stopped. Rising up on her knees a bit more, the tip of her tongue circled the head of his throbbing member and then her lips opened fully and took the length of him into her warm, moist mouth.

"Oh. My. God."

Sucking. Licking. Alternating motions as her fingers splayed across his ass, digging into the muscles in the most exquisite pain Rob had ever experienced. His hips tried to rock, but with near brutal strength she held him still as she continued her manipulations until he screamed as an orgasm took him over the edge of sanity into pure, primal need.

GENTLY, ADELINE RAN her tongue up the length of the intoxicating man's cock until it popped out, still rigid but definitely spent. Wow. She hadn't been that turned on by giving a man a blow job...ever. So much for taking it slow.

His hands had braced behind him while she'd licked and sucked, but now were tangled in her hair. One came down to cup her chin, turning her face up to look into those amazing eyes, golden and flecked with color like tiger eye's jewels. "Oh. My. God. That was amazing." His entire body still shook.

"Glad you liked it." She licked her lips and noticed his eyes grow wide and darken. Adeline pushed herself up, rising on her toes to suck on his lower lip before turning around abruptly. "What do you have to drink around here?"

The one-room studio apartment was a disaster. Clothes strewn on the floor, back of a chair, and across the unmade bed. The kitchen counter was cluttered with kitchen appliances and two opened boxes of cereal. *Not the neatest cad in town.*

Behind her she heard the sounds of Rob pulling up his pants. "I'm sure there's something suitable. Here, take a seat," he pulled out one of the kitchen chairs and dusted off the table, "I'll tend to you." The way his voice grew husky on those last words sent a wave of pulsating heat down to her groin. Adeline hoped he wasn't just talking about the drink now.

Rob opened up a cabinet, empty except for a couple bottles of liquor. A minute later, he handed her a tumbler with deep amber liquid and a couple ice cubes. "Hope you like it. I'm afraid I'm out of the good stuff."

Raising the glass to her lips, his eyes closely watching her face, she tilted the glass back to allow the beverage to slowly slide down her throat, leaving a burning trail tasting of cinnamon and whiskey. "Yum. What do you call this creation?"

Rob face lit up, as the corners of his mouth quirked up in a devilish grin. "Well, to be honest, I just threw together some Jack Daniels with a shot of Goldslogger. Doesn't have a name yet, as far as I know, so you may have the honor of naming it."

Adeline pursed her lips to think for a moment. "How about ... Fool's Gold?"

He tossed back his own drink, slammed the glass on the table, and let loose a hearty, deep-throated laugh. "Perfect."

His eyes roved up and down her body as the laughter died. "My God, you are perfect." The words barely a whisper.

Goosebumps erupted across her skin. Even his voice penetrated to her core as deep as a kiss. Taking a moment to collect her thoughts, Adeline cleared her throat before attempting to speak. "So, I'm guessing we don't need to worry about a roommate walking in?" Her hands waved around the tiny space.

His face broke out in a wide grin. "Nope. No roomie."

"So ... you're a lone wolf then?" The laughter dimmed in his topaz eyes for just a moment, so brief Adeline doubted she saw it at all.

"Guess so. Been on my own since forever. I prefer it that way." The grim set of his mouth sent a wave of regret through her own heart. She knew exactly what being a loner meant, and the unspoken toll it took on one's soul.

"Yeah, I get it. Bit of a loner myself." She'd meant the words to come out cavalier and carefree but heard the sadness in her own raspy voice. The way he gazed back at her, it was evident he recognized the sentiment.

Without warning, he grabbed her hand and pulled her onto his lap. His hand reached up to cup her cheek. The pad of his thumb caressed her skin as it wiped away a tear she hadn't even felt rise up and fall from her eyes. Breath caught in her lungs, fighting against the involuntary threatening sob. "It's okay, sweet Adeline," he whispered before claiming her mouth with his. The kiss sent waves of pleasure through her, unleashing the pent-up loneliness she'd held back for so long and slaying it into a thousand shards of glass.

Rob pulled back from the kiss. Instinctively, her arms wrapped tightly around him. The small separation of their bodies left her chilled. His heated breath against the curve of her neck, Rob's lips found her sensitive spot, just under her ear. Moaning, she arched to give him greater access to her neck as her hands roamed across his solid chest. Despite the outward appearance of a tech geek, this man was all brawn underneath and she yearned for more of him. All of him.

The deep aching had her squirming in his lap as he nibbled on her ear lobe. One hand roughly pushed aside her silk blouse and cupped her breast, squeezing while enticing her nipple to harden almost painfully with the pad of his thumb over the lace of her bra. A growl started in her chest and built up until it escaped her lips.

HUNTED

Adeline fisted Rob's hair, pulling his face to hers. "Time for you to take care of me," she breathed against his mouth.

19

Chapter 3

With the fluid movements of a panther, Rob scooped her up in his arms, stood, and carried her over to the unmade king-sized bed that filled the tiny space. He stumbled once over a pile of clothes but managed not to drop her. Gently, he laid her down on the soft, t-shirt cotton sheets. The material was cold against Adeline's heated skin. He stepped back and gazed down at her with eyes darkened to a burnt umber hue. Light from a streetlamp streamed in through the open Venetian blinds to cast a halo around his already golden-haired head. Just staring up at him, Adeline's body tensed with unfulfilled need. Her arms reached up to pull him down on top of her, but his lips curled wickedly to one side, highlighting his dimples.

Shaking his head, a chuckle rumbled from his throat. "Patience is a virtue." Then, leaning down, he whispered, "It's your turn, remember. Just relax and let me take *care* of you." Adeline's muscles clenched down low, sending tremors up her body as she instinctively reached for him again. Every ounce of her wanted his cock inside her, filling her. Now. She'd been patient long enough. Months of not hunting, not succumbing to her primal needs. Adeline wanted what she wanted, and she wanted him thrusting deep into her quaking core.

Adeline's wrists were captured in one large, strong hand that pinned her arms above her head. He tisked through clenched teeth. "I said ... patience. It will be worth your while, I promise. Now," his other hand grasped her chin forcing her to look directly into his eyes, "... are you going to be a good girl?"

She bit her lower lip but nodded. The emerald flecks in his hazel eyes danced at her silent agreement. Adeline wanted to drown in those eyes and never resurface. There was a hidden peace in them that called to something else within her. Something unbidden. A yearning for something long denied.

Rob dipped his head to where their faces were barely an inch apart, paused for a split second before closing the gap, brushing his lips against hers like a feather floating across bare skin. The hold on her wrists relaxed as he deepened the kiss, playfully luring her lips to part. A sigh escaped, whether hers or his she couldn't tell anymore as they breathed and moved in unison. Then ... fresh blast of artic air as he moved off her body to stand again.

"What. The. Hell?"

Again, the playful grin and shake of the head. "If I kiss you anymore, you'll have me cum'ing again before I ever get a chance to satisfy you. Can't have that." Glancing down, his arousal was evident as a bulge strained against the fabric of his jeans.

"Well, it wasn't my idea for you to put your pants back on. Frankly, I object to their very existence." Even to her own ears, her voice sounded husky like a kitten purring.

Without answering, Rob moved aside the flimsy blouse material still barely draped over her torso. "My God, you're beautiful." The pupils of his eyes dilated as one finger tugged the offending garment away to reveal more of her. His other hand pulled her to a sitting position, and the blouse cascaded down her arms. Kneeling, they were face to face, eyes locked on each other while he confidently reached around to unclasp her ivory lace bra with a single flick of his thumb. Just the slightest graze of his skin against hers sent pulsating waves of heat through her limbs as another purr rumbled from her chest.

His head dipped, breaking eye contact and leaving Adeline a view of a blanket of dark golden curls in disarray. The same breathy kiss from before, but this time against the delicate skin of her neck. She squirmed as the tip of his tongue tickled down her neck, lingered over her clavicle, tracing it like an artist outlining his subject in charcoal. One hand planted on one side of her, the other came up to cup her naked breast, rubbing agonizing circles around one nipple before pinching it slightly.

Her own head fell back as a wave of pleasure rocketed from the breast down to her throbbing wet pussy. What had he said earlier about cum'ing ahead of time? That was close to being her. She wasn't completely undressed yet and an orgasm threatened to engulf her. *It's been a while since the last time, but this man has ...* and the thought vanished, followed by another shock of ecstasy when his hot, mouth clamped down on her other breast, sucking with his lips and flicking his tongue against the nipple. "Oh. My." Adeline's body shuddered before the final exclamation could escape.

Suddenly, cold air ensconced her again as he pulled back. Her hands free, she pulled his face down to her own. "Fuck me. Now," she panted. He hadn't even touched her needy, wet core and she was a breath away from the most rocking climax of her life.

A howl of rage almost broke from her lungs as he shook his head again. "I'm nowhere near done with you yet." She could use her wolf strength and take back control, but all ideas of resistance fled when he pushed her back against the mattress and held her there with one hand. The other hand fumbled briefly with her pants button and zipper before shucking the garment down her legs with her moistened silk panties scrunched inside. All the while, his eyes held her gaze. "Stay still," he warned while releasing his hold on her upper body.

Warm, slightly rough hands caressed her curves, while his lips trailed down her chest, stopping briefly at her navel before venturing further down. Reaching under her, Rob hosted her legs up and pushed them wider as he knelt down. For a moment, nothing happened. Adeline imagined he was trying to process how she had the same white, nearly metallic silver hair there.

An appreciative groan echoed in the room. "You. Are. Beautiful." His hands trailed down her thighs to rest in the "V" of her hips and pelvis, his long fingers massaging around her folds as his breath tickled against her sensitive skin.

Her hips bucked, urging him to explore more of her. "Please …"

At first, the movement was so slight it barely registered as his thumbs grazed against her swollen lips and gently pushed their way in between. Still grasping her pelvis with his fingers, the thumbs explored first before giving way to the heat and expertise of his tongue. One flick against her clit and Adeline writhed, panting, unable to control her own body any longer. The teasing was pure torture. Exquisite in its pleasure and pain.

Hands held her down, stopping her movements. "Not yet," he breathed against her cunt just as his tongue flicked out again, encircling her nub before fastening on it with his lips to suck, then lavish with his tongue again.

"Oh ... please." She begged, her climax building and building, but he wouldn't let her unleash it yet. Adeline had never allowed anyone to control her like this, not in any way, much less sexually.

As his mouth and tongue continued their ministrations, and as Adeline struggled not to howl, one of his thumbs penetrated, pushing against her from the inside while he tortured her externally. A scream wrenched from deep within as the earth shattered around her, leaving her spasming against the sheets and quivering under his lips.

Several moments passed, as the climax rocked her and Rob held her against his face, his fingers digging into her clenched buttocks as her hips rocked back and forth wildly. The tremors subsided before he emerged from between her legs, a smile plastered on his slick lips. Shaking his head, he knelt over her until he was just an inch or less from her face. "Don't get too comfortable. I'm not finished yet."

ROB WATCHED THE BEAUTIFUL woman curled up beside him as her chest rose and fell with her slumbered breaths. A tiny cross necklace lay against her ivory skin, the chain pooling between her breasts.

This night, and morning, had been the wildest of his life. He'd started the evening out, washing down the needles of guilt from his crime with a couple draft beers. Even stealing from a self-serving bastard politician left a vile taste in his mouth. Never in a million years had he thought he'd be swept away by a wildfire of desire that burned every other thought and feeling to a crisp.

He blinked. Had it all been real? As soon as those resplendent eyes had locked on his, there had only been pure, unadulterated lust raging through his veins. Nice, seeing as it had been months since he'd allowed himself the distraction of a woman in his life. The last one had slammed out of his apartment in a huff, but he'd barely noticed. He'd been focused on one thing. Revenge.

But this amazing woman awakened something buried deep within him. Something primal, long denied but never completely vanished. He'd been content being on his own, but now the idea of releasing Adeline from his arms … it gutted him.

The past few hours had been mind-blowing. In more ways than one. Yes, the sex … Oh. My. God. The sex! The silver-maned beauty oozed sexuality from the moment she'd slid into the seat across from him at the pub. But nothing would have prepared him for the wild ride she'd given him. He felt the corners of his mouth tick up … or the ride he gave her back.

Hours later, he'd lost count of how many times they'd pleasured each other. No matter how hard they climaxed, within minutes they were ready for more. Never had he experienced anything like this. He couldn't get enough of her. It was like a moth being drawn to the flame, singed, and then going back for more.

The pedestal sink in the bathroom hadn't survived. After fumbling with the water cut-off, Adeline had grabbed his hand and pulled him through the water to the kitchen where they'd resumed their activities on a more stable surface. Later, the towel rack had crashed down on the cold tile from another go in the bathroom as she'd clutched it for support while her legs encircled his waist and he'd plunged into her with every ounce of strength he had.

Would he ever experience another night like this one again? Perhaps not, but he'd die happy knowing he'd had last night. Then again, he didn't think he could let Adeline go.

Laying on the mussed bed, his fingers absently trailed up and down her arm. Goosebumps broke out in their path. Even the tiny hairs on her arms held a metallic silver sheen as the early morning light gently touched her skin. A soft growl escaped her still swollen lips. Not a warning sound, but a welcoming guttural groan.

Adeline rolled towards him and opened her eyes. Her pupils were dilated, mirroring a darkened image of himself. A sleepy smile flashed, and then... she was on top of him, legs straddling his naked hips. He was more than ready as she slid her wet pussy down his shaft, slowly. Halfway down, she squeezed back up, letting the top of his penis flick out of her. He didn't have to look to know white cum already oozed out of the tip.

Her smile widened and she reached behind, her fingers cupped his balls and gave a slight squeeze. She lowered herself again. This time, not allowing him to penetrate her, just letting her wet folds caress his cock. Up and down, slowly. Agonizing slowly.

Dear Lord, hadn't they both just cum not even half an hour ago. Oh, who the fuck cares ...

Her rhythm picked up, still rubbing her clit along his shaft. He needed to plunge deep into her, but then the exquisite ecstasy would soon end. Adeline moaned and arched her back as her nails gently scratched along his testicles. The sound of her building to her orgasm, guttural moans mixed with higher-pitched sighs, ricocheted in his eardrums, adding to his own body's demands.

Unable to take the torture any longer, Rob grabbed her delicate hips and held her in place. Her dripping cunt hovered above the tip of his cock. For a second, their eyes met. A slight nod of her head. Still gripping her hip bones, her plunged into her and they released simultaneously screams.

Moments later, both still trembling, he wrapped his arms around her, closed his eyes. A sweet darkness took him.

Chapter 4

A red hue burned her eyelids. Morning already? Ugh. Adeline groaned. Her body ached all over. She attempted to push herself up, then realized she was trapped by a muscular arm draped over her chest, and a mass of curls snuggled into the nape of her neck.

Oh. Yeah. Rob. Yum.

She couldn't hold back the smile as thoughts of the previous night rampaged through her brain. That had been ... nice. Well, nice was not exactly the most appropriate word, but she realized she was still too "fucked dumb" to elicit a more appropriate term. Her brain would kick in after she extricated herself from the handsome god she'd landed last night. With their bodies still touching, the only true thought coursing through her was whether or not to wake him up *properly*.

Who had been the hunter and who had been the prey last night? She'd started the night looking for easy quarry to satisfy her primal needs, and he had definitely succeeded there. However, the warm and fuzzy feeling wrapped around her body like a quilt made her feel less of a predator in the aftermath. She'd been caught unawares by his own vulnerability, that for a second the veil covering her own had been pulled aside.

An unfamiliar sensation of comfort, peace, and home settled in heart. A bit scary, but at the same time...not. Those strong, sculpted arms belonged around her. Had she allowed herself to be captured? When had the tables turned? An ache built up in her chest. Eventually, she'd have to eradicate herself from his embrace, probably never to return again. For a little longer, Adeline vowed...just a little bit longer.

A soft buzzing penetrated the quiet. *What's that noise?* After a few seconds, it stopped. *Ah, my phone. Crap, what did I miss?*

Like ice water thrown on the burning embers of a bonfire, reality smashed in. Slowly, Adeline wiggled until she could reach the edge of the bed and slid off soundlessly.

She fumbled around for her clothes and her phone. After shucking her arms into the sleeve of her blouse, her fingers tapped the phone screen. Four missed calls; just as many text messages. All from her partner, Vincent.

A soft snore rose from the vicinity of the bed, distracting her. She stumbled trying to get one leg into her pants, knocking over a tiny trash can sticking out from underneath the round Formica table in the middle of the room. Heat crept up her face recalling all the deeds done on top of that table just a few hours ago.

She tapped the screen again to read the texts while her other hand picked up the trash can.

Where are you? Boss wants update.

Nothing here.

Everyone checks out, but there's one sub-contractor MIA.

APB put out for this dude. He hasn't been heard from in over 24 hours.

Followed by a picture.

Staring back at her from the phone was a golden blonde, curly headed man, with five o'clock shadow making his face even more ruggedly handsome, and hazel eyes framed by wire-rimmed glasses. Adeline's stomach sank. Her hand flew to her mouth to stifle a gasp.

No. Can't be.

The phone vibrated in her hand again. Her thumb crushed the button on the side to send the call to voicemail. Her mouth dry and fingers trembling, Adeline tapped out... *Following a lead. Back to you in half hour.*

Figures. She'd just experienced the most mind-blowing sexual experience of her life. Their connection transcended the physical. Of that, she was certain.

So of course, there would be a catch.

She glanced back at the Adonis slumbering in the bed. Even unconscious, he was gorgeous, and a familiar longing rose up from deep within her. He'd done a good job hiding his utter masculine appearance with the super-casual clothes and the glasses, but she'd seen the truth even before she'd reached his table at the bar last night. There was no denying the physicality of the man, and her animal instincts were never wrong. However, she hadn't dubbed him as a criminal at first sight.

Getting slow, Addy.

It was that or her sex-starved body wouldn't let her see the truth. She was renowned in the Agency for sniffing out crooks within seconds of meeting them. But this...she hadn't seen coming.

Tugging on the rest of her clothes, her eyes scanned the room. Rob had been glued to his laptop before her arrival at his table. Now where was the damn thing?

Please don't let it still be at the bar.

No, she distinctly remembered the satchel slung across his back when they'd walked out.

What about after the alley where they'd dived out of the sight of patrol car?

There's your clue, girlfriend. Hiding from the cops. Duh!

No, the laptop made it back to the apartment. Vaguely, she recalled the clunking sound it made when the bag had slid to the floor, along with Rob's pants, when they first arrived.

Another gentle snore broke her concentration. She'd have to be quick. Of course, this could also constitute unlawful search and seizure if she did find anything. Considering the means to which she came about to discover any evidence would be prime for a defense attorney's arguments to dismiss. Not to mention, Agent Vinny the Annoying would most certainly be taking over her spot as the Agency kicked her ass to the curb for her behavior.

Never mind. Just do your damn job. Worry about the rest when we get to that. Hey, he may not even be guilty of anything!

Adeline's gut coiled like a spring. Now that instinct, non-primal sexual instinct, had taken back over, she knew the truth already.

Rob wasn't being coy when he claimed to be a lone wolf. He was *The Lone Wolf.*

Tiptoeing over to the door, she retrieved the laptop bag and eased the computer out. The screen was cracked in a couple places, but it burst to life as if it hadn't been shut down probably, just put to sleep. A *Heavy Metal 2000* screensaver popped up, complete with an animated woman with huge tits bursting out of a red corset (bare except for thin strings covering the sensitive parts) with a machete in one hand and a grenade launcher in the other.

Classic geek.

A few soft pecks on the keyboard, she cracked his passcode in seconds. She checked all the files. Most were encrypted, but she wasn't the best at her job for nothing. A few taps on the computer and it was all laid bare.

Adeline dove into the source code. Nothing raised a red flag, except for the lack of red flags. A hacker always had his or her personal stamp when they committed a hack. Even the best. Obviously, she had yet to discover his calling card.

He had been glued to the monitor at the bar. Obviously, he was looking at something important then. Why couldn't she find it now? He hadn't even booted the computer down properly. There simply had to be something hiding in plain sight.

Emails? All benign. Mostly spam. No outgoing emails. No social media accounts. Normally, that would be an indicator, but who was she to judge? Adeline avoided Facebook and all that other garbage, too.

Music files? Of course. She clicked on the folder labeled "Heavy Metal" and found exactly what she was looking for and had been near desperate not to find. Hidden in between the sound files was a code indiscernible to most, but her analytical brain had long ago found hacking to be as easy as tracking a wounded and bleeding fugitive in the snow. Another touch of the keyboard and her worst fears were revealed. Her gut twisted and bile rose in her throat.

She snagged her phone to take screen shots of everything. A map laid out in code. It was all there, linking the hunk in the bed to the case she was working. But something else caught her eye – news articles about a mass killing of an extended family in rural Tennessee. Actually, most of the small community had been found slaughtered. The name of the town struck a faint memory, but she couldn't quite grasp the reason for it.

One article title stood out, "Youngest Son of Town's Mayor Missing, Not Amongst the Dead." A black and white photo of a lanky boy with a mop full of curls on top of head and familiar eyes. The same eyes she'd witnessed last night when they'd flashed with interest, and then dimmed in sadness just for a moment. The article described how the town had suffered many suspicious deaths over a period of months, residents falling mysteriously ill. Then later, a lost hiker stumbled upon what remained of the town where mutilated bodies had been piled up, set on fire, and were still smoldering. Another article, an obituary for the hiker, was also in the files. The poor guy died a couple weeks later of anaphylactic shock. The doctors were baffled by his sudden onset of severe allergy to eggs.

Adeline couldn't feel any worse than if she'd been kicked in the stomach. *Can't let your emotions get in the way, Addy. He's a criminal.* She wiped a tear away and focused back on the more incriminating hacking feats he'd accomplished.

For being such an excellent hacker – the way he infiltrated the systems and got out was mind-boggling – why had he not destroyed his own hard drive, dumped the computer into the river, and driven off into the sunset? Did the jerk want to be caught?

"What ya doing, beautiful?"

Adeline froze, finger hovering above the keyboard of Rob's laptop.

Maybe all that sex did mess with her brain because she hadn't heard him stir from the bed. Now he was standing over her, still naked and fully erect, with an anxious expression.

"Uh ..."

A loud shattering sound reverberated through the apartment. Shards of glass cascaded over them both like a waterfall. Adeline had no time to react, much less to shift into her animal form in defense. Soldiers clothed completely in black invaded the room from the broken windows and the now smashed in flimsy wooden door. Rob's voice rose above the clamor, "What. The ..." followed by silence as one soldier punched him squarely in the face and he fell to the ground.

Growling, she launched herself at Rob's assailant only to be yanked back by her hair. A soldier restrained her with both arms around her chest. Another stood directly in front of her, his face hidden by black SWAT equipment. She sensed the action before he swung but was too late to avoid his large fist.

Pain shot through her skull as blood poured down her face. "You ... bast..."

Darkness enveloped her.

Chapter 5

Infernal ringing in her ears slammed through Adeline's head. *What the hell?* But if she thought the sound was bad, opening her eyes made that a walk in the park. A blaring spotlight shone directly into her face. A chill permeated her skin from the metal flooring as she squirmed and wiggled to a sitting position.

"Glad to see you could join us, Agent Marion."

She'd know that smarmy voice anywhere. Irritation raced through her body in increasing waves, threatening to bring forth her wolf.

"Vinny," she growled, "If you wanted my attention so bad, there are more subtle, less painful ways of going about it."

Although she couldn't see through the glaring light, Adeline could clearly make out his silhouette on one side of the lamp and another taller figure on the other side. She pulled at the zip ties binding her hands behind her back, desperately wanting to wipe hair out of her eyes. Thankfully, they had not used handcuffs.

"Come on, Vin. You really think it's necessary to cuff me? I'm the good guy, remember?" She trained her voice to come off steady and assured, but her insides quaked. Fear. Not a familiar emotion, but something was deadly wrong about this situation. Evil permeated the very air, a rotten egg sulphuric odor. *Demons?*

Here? She would've picked that up from her partner earlier if he were demonic unless it was a recent possession.

"Miss Marion," a distinct voice, oddly familiar addressed her. "It seems you've been hanging around the wrong people. Not appropriate for a federal agent to be cohorting with treasonous criminals." A tremor ran down her spine.

Senator Johnson?

"Senator, good to finally meet you. Congratulations on your re-election last time. Heard that was a close one. Considering the big kahuna's job next, I hear." Too late, her sarcasm and disrespect for authority had opened her mouth before her brain caught up to the danger of her situation.

A deep throaty chuckle echoed around the room. Sniffing the air again, Adeline detected cold metal. No concrete, no carpet or tile. No wood, brick, or mortar. Metal. The way the echo quickly died, she assumed it was a small metal room, possibly a vault.

"I like her, Vincent. Where have you been keeping this gem?"

The answering gruff wasn't flattering. "More trouble than she's worth. Damn good at her job though."

For a moment the light was blocked as his lithe figure moved towards her, his hand grabbing her chin to tilt her face up. "But she did find the bad guy in record time. Told you she has a nose for detective work. However, I was surprised Agent Marion's judgment led her to sleep with the miscreant. A girl must have her fun, I guess. Isn't that right, sweetheart?" His fingers chucked her chin to the side before he stepped back.

Adeline fought the urge to rip her wrists out of the zip ties. *Honestly, zip ties? Anyone can get out of those. What was he thinking?* She needed to play along to see what exactly her partner and the senator were up to. Couldn't wait too much longer, the binds were burning her wrists like they'd been laced with some caustic substance.

"Ah, I bet you're wondering if you can get out of those bindings faster than I can pull my gun on you." He knelt in front of her now on one knee, his breath warmed her face, minty with a hint of hops but no sulphur.

Unblinking, she locked eyes with him. She knew in the darkness her silver eyes shone, a warning to prey. With the spotlight blinding her, she also knew that the effect was lost. "Just wondering *why* my hands are bound. Like you said, I found the bad guy for you. Not exactly the promotion I was aiming for with this case. Would you like to explain to the good senator why you have me all tied up, cuz I'd love to know myself?"

"I'm sorry, my dear, for the restraints. We couldn't be certain of your loyalties considering the state you were found in with the hacker. I must say, it didn't look like you were on the hunt for a criminal. Perhaps you were hunting for something else when you stumbled upon him?" The senator's gravelly tone resounded in the room. Pretty good assumption on his part. That was exactly what happened.

Glancing up, she noticed he still maintained his distance near the lamp. "What can I say? Perhaps I like to play with my prey before going for the kill." Now to get the conversation back onto him, and less on her sex life. Obviously, the situation with the hacker stealing money and siphoning intelligence to the media was more complex than originally thought. Otherwise, Rob would be cuffed and booked already, and she'd be giving a statement uptown, not hidden away in a steel vault somewhere.

"Um, by the way, where is the jailbird? Got him locked away in a different vault or did you execute him immediately?"

Her stomach lurched at the thought of gorgeous, sweet Rob lying in a ditch somewhere, a bullet to the back of his head, or sinking to the bottom of the Potomac as fish nibbled on his once radiant eyes. Considering the situation she found herself in, a mafia-style execution wasn't too far outside the spectrum of possibility. But why?

"None of your damn business ..." Vincent's tone dripped like acid in her ear before he was interrupted by the smoother senator.

"Now, Vincent. No need for hostility. I'm sure Agent Marion here will be more than happy to help us with our investigation so we can recover all my money. Right, dear?" He'd moved rather quickly for a sixty-something man as he now stood beside her, his hand reached and grabbed her forearm, dragging her to her feet. She stumbled as she found her footing. The senator pulled a chair out of the darkness and waved for her to take a seat.

"Right, sir. Whatever I can do to help." Adeline fought her primal instincts to lash out with her legs to kick them both in the balls. Her inner wolf wanted to shred their throats until their dead bodies ceased to buck and shake as death took hold. Instead, she forced her sweetest smile and tone of voice. If they went to all this trouble to keep her and Rob from the actual authorities, perhaps she could coax more damaging information from them before executing an escape.

"Excellent. Vincent, why don't you retrieve our other guest?" As Vinny left the room, the senator towered over her a bit too closely. There it was. Just under the designer cologne of bergamot and cinnamon ... Sulphur.

Well, she'd always known DC brought out the worst sorts, but an honest-to-evilness demon? Wow.

"Now, dear," the endearment gnawed at her patience, "I do apologize for the treatment you've received. However, I'm afraid it's only going to be worse from here on out. It would behoove you to cooperate in *every* way. I have the power to make things go smoothly and quite painlessly for you ... or make things incredibly uncomfortable and outright torturous." His weathered face inches from her own, Adeline fought the urge to flinch away from the wicked gleam in his crimson-tinged eyes.

"Gee, Senator. I don't know. Seems I am not often subjected to dealing with demons unless I'm ripping them to bloody shreds." Her canine teeth elongated in her mouth, pricking her own tongue as Adeline craned her neck to look up at the senator. *Keep it together, Addy. Don't provoke him too much. Not until you know if Rob is safe.*

"Ah, I surmised as such. That you knew. You're a smart woman, or should I say wolf?" His hand reached out to caress her cheek. Adeline felt the prickles as hair sprouted from her skin as the wolf fought to gain control of her body in order to protect herself. "Haven't seen your kind in the metropolitan area in decades. I was confident that we annihilated them all."

Adeline inhaled deeply to tamp down the inner beast. "New to town."

"New to the entire east coast, I'd imagined. It took us decades, but I guarantee the wolf shifters on this side of the continent are indeed extinct. The ones hiding out West will be soon as well." He backed away and shook his head. "Well, unless you want to petrify the poor young man you so recently fucked, you'll calm down and lose the furry look. Doesn't do your complexion any favors either."

The door creaked open, without even a glimmer of light to mark where the door actually was. Total blackness behind it. With a resonating slam, followed by the softest click as a lock took hold. A large form was thrown down in front of her, landing on her toes with a grunt.

Vincent stepped forward and kicked the man huddled on the floor. "Wake up, asshat! Time to talk."

EVERY MUSCLE ACHED as if he'd been in a meat grinder and spit out the other side. But he was alive. He was painfully aware that he was indeed alive. Rob attempted to sit up, but found his hands still bound behind his back. However, there was something else in the room that caught his attention. A strong female scent, a little woodsy mixed with citrus. *They got Adeline, too.*

"Let her go. She has nothing to do with this," he croaked despite the sandpaper sensation in his throat. His assailant answered merely with another rib-cracking kick, so agonizing that he could only gasp for breath.

"Too late, buddy. You already got her locked into your guilt. Didn't anyone ever tell you *guilty by association*? Considering how much associating you two have been up to ..."

"Shut the fuck up, Vinny! Leave him alone." Adeline's voice was music to his ears, but he wished more than anything they'd never met. She didn't deserve to deal with his mess.

Rob wiggled around on the floor until he could maneuver to face her. "Adeline, I'm so sorry. I'll get you out of this, I promise." And he meant every word. He wasn't clear on the details of how he would do that, but he would. Even if it meant losing the veneer of the placid computer geek to show his true, more violent self – the one he'd purposefully kept hidden for years.

A throaty chuckle drew his attention to the dark form standing behind Adeline, just on the cusp of the shadows. "Mr. Holden, seems you've been a very bad boy. And dragging the damsel into this ... tsk, tsk, tsk."

"I'm not a damsel ..." Adeline's words were cut off by an ear-splitting slap.

"Not your turn to talk, bitch!"

Rob launched himself at her attacker, the man that had brought him into the room. The same man who had been using him as a punching bag for the last three hours. He collided with him, knocking him down, but without use of his arms and hands, he was weaponless. Within seconds, the man ... what was his name, Vinny? ... was using him as a kickball again.

The crunch of his own bones thrummed in his ears. The coppery taste of his blood filled his mouth fueling the anger already building deep in his core. He didn't know how much longer he could hold out.

He rolled over and spat blood at Vinny's highly polished dress shoes.

"Ready to have a proper conversation now or do you prefer to be treated like a mangy dog?" That voice. That arrogant, nasally, shout-whisper voice akin to what he imagined Kiefer Sutherland would sound like if he were as old as Yoda. He knew that voice.

"Senator? Didn't think you'd get your own hands dirty. I thought Mr. Nottingham did all that for you. Couldn't get him to fly in from his vacation in the Alps this time to clean up after you?"

"Mr. Holden, let me be blunt with you. Either you return my money, every cent, and you sign a document stating that everything you illegally released to the media was false and you made the whole thing up, or ..." Suddenly, the senator was standing over him. His eyes flared with a mysterious red tinge. "... or your lady friend here dies a horrendous death in front of your eyes. And that's not the best part." His lips curled up in a wicked smile, displaying all his pearly white teeth. "Your fingerprints will be found all over her. You've already accomplished that part. Then, your own bloody signature will be added to the document as your suicide note."

Anger boiled in his gut. If it were just him, he'd tell the bastard to go to hell. But Adeline ... sweet Adeline. He couldn't allow her to be hurt. Something sparked deep within him, a need to protect what was his. No matter what happened to him, he'd keep her safe. They'd only known each other a few hours, but one thing he knew for a fact was that Adeline was worth dying for, was worth everything.

His own lips opened and moved as if to speak, but he couldn't form the words to surrender. It wasn't in his nature. Fight, not flight, was his course. It always had been. Even after he'd hacked the system, moved the money, and released the damaging information, he'd known they would hunt him down to the ends of the Earth.

It was the information hidden within the snippets he'd passed along to the media that were the most damning. Taxpayer dollars being rerouted from a Nottingham, Inc. work order to assist in establishing refugee settlements to the senator's personal accounts. That was the least of the senator's sins. What the money did fund... well, that was the true story, and it was an ugly one. There would be no favorable political spin on that tale. All the horrific deeds accomplished by Nottingham, Inc. with the senator's full approval and backing – slaughtering hundreds of wolf shifters, and anyone else who got in their way, in order to build their own sweatshops hidden away in the outskirts of Tennessee. And not just little children making cheap clothes. No, it was so much worse.

The idea of fleeing had crossed his mind, only for a second. He'd been sitting at that bar, contemplating that very thing when Adeline had approached him. That had been the last he'd considered running. All that beautiful, flowing silver hair and matching metallic eyes had glued him in place. Deep down, he knew then what resounded through his body now...he'd fight for her. To be near her. To hold her. To love her. He wouldn't sacrifice her to the senator or to anyone.

Rob glanced over to Adeline. The lack of fear in her eyes and expression surprised him, but also gave him hope. She shook her head and mouthed, "No."

In response, all the anger and fear rampaging through his veins lit on fire. His pores opened, releasing course reddish-gold hairs. Blood tickled his tongue as sharp fangs protruded from his gums. Bones crunched. Skin stretched. All painfully, but also with a feeling of familiarity and comfort. Rob Holden may not be capable of saving a fly, but his wolf could do much, much more.

Chapter 6

Adeline's eyes flew wide and then she blinked a number of times. There was no way she was seeing what she was seeing. The hottest computer geek she'd ever laid eyes on was morphing into something not human ... hairs sprouted from every pore; his perfectly chiseled jaw elongated; fingernails grew into long, sharp claws behind his back as his wrists were still bound. Just hours ago, she'd run her hands and her mouth over most of this man's exquisite body. A man no longer.

The zip ties snapped loudly, the sound muffled only by the cracking of bones and moans of agony as Rob continued to transform. Adeline's breath caught in her chest. Rob was a shifter, too? How was that possible? She should've caught on to that immediately. It wasn't like wolves could hide their true scent from others of their kind. Disguise it from humans ... sure. But a wolf could always sniff out a wolf.

Vincent and the senator stood paralyzed a few feet away. A new scent permeated the stagnant vault air ... fear.

Now on all fours, Rob's wolf turned blazing topaz eyes on her. The beast lifted its snout and sniffed before nodding in understanding. If they lived through this, they needed to have a serious conversation.

How had she not known?

Well, the gig is up now. Might as well join the party.

Deep down in her very soul, Adeline released her own primal animal, set her free, as Rob backed their captors into a corner. Saliva dripped from his maw and a guttural rumble erupted from his chest.

Hairs sprang up along her arms and legs, racing from her limbs to her core, then up her neck. Shaking her head, Adeline's mane of silver hair grew course as shorter strands burgeoned along her scalp and began to form along her face.

But something was wrong. Her bones should be snapping and reforming. Her face should transform from its feminine human form to that of a majestic she-wolf, but…it wasn't. Slowly, even her fur receded back into her skin.

A cackle filled the room, startling everyone, including Rob's wolf who ceased growling. He craned his neck around to peer at her.

"My dear," the senator's deep voice hitched as he feigned an attempt to stop his laughter, "having a little pest control problem, are you?"

Anger spread through her veins. Her wolf was captured. Restrained by forces she didn't understand. What had the demonic politician done to her?

Senator Johnson stepped out to the side, away from Rob's startled wolf. In the spotlight, his gluttonous features cast freaky shadows across his face, giving his normally ruddy cheeks and deep-set eyes a malevolent manifestation like a gargoyle statue. "You see, my dear, we knew about your little *condition* and took precautions, but this one …" he shrugged in the wolf's direction, "was a surprise."

Adeline's lips opened to ask the question, "How?" but her vocal cords were shocked into silence.

The senator's lips curled up, revealing his full set of teeth. "Your bindings, dear. Laced them with something special. Nothing that would overtly hurt you like silver. Just a little leash."

A snarl, then a sharp bark turned her attention back to Rob. His head swiveled between the senator and Vincent who still stood with his back against the wall, his eyes bulging from their sockets. Rivulets of sweat streamed down his face. A tiny movement caught her eye. Vinny's fingers tapped along his waist.

"Gun!" Adeline scrambled to her feet and leaped over the wolf. She slammed into Vinny just as his hand pulled the gun from around the small of his back. The collision knocked it out of his grip and the weapon clanged across the metal floor.

Her wrists still bound, she did the only thing she could…repeatedly, and with great force, thrust her knee into Vinny's nuts as she lay on top of him. The acrid stench of fear wafted off him. Rob growled behind her, waiting on his chance to rip the man apart. Unable to do more damage to him, she rolled off and the wolf pounced.

A COPPERY TASTE FILLED his mouth, both sweet and repulsive. It'd been so long since Rob tasted blood. He'd gone to great lengths to tamp the inner beast down. As the fur receded and the wolf became dormant, a mixture of disgust and sorrow filled his heart.

A gasp pulled his attention away from the heap of ripped human in front of him. Rob pivoted around and his stomach sank even further. Adeline. Beautiful Adeline. A woman he could have never resisted in a million years. She was the reason he hadn't run away, left town, and never looked back.

The spotlight refracted in her metallic eyes reminding him of how jewelry stores set up showcase lighting to best reveal the glimmer of precious metals and stones. He couldn't bear the idea of her not only glimpsing the real him, but having to watch his beast at his worst, killing.

"Adeline, I'm..."

A soft click echoed off the walls. Although he couldn't see the weapon, he knew the senator held a gun on Adeline. Her large almond eyes narrowed into slits and a nerve twitched along her jawline. She wasn't afraid. Amazing. No, she was pissed.

"Mr. Holden, I must say you've shocked us all tonight. I only thought to deal with an insignificant hacker. Easy peasy. Then the added complication of Agent Marion, but this was most unexpected." The senator's chuckle sounded more like a wolverine clearing its throat of bad carrion than a laugh.

"Let her go." Rob made to lunge forward, but a quick look at Adeline froze him in place.

No. You'll play into his hands. Just wait.

Her melodic voice inside his head. How was that possible? Only other wolf shifters could ...

No. Couldn't be.

An image swam in his head. Something his wolf had witnessed. Her beautiful silver hair growing longer, covering more of her body. The silver glint in her eyes morphing into an icy predatory gleam.

"Quite the lovely couple you two make. Too bad neither of you will live to make puppies together. Would've been a beautiful litter." Although Rob couldn't see the old man, two red eyes blazed through the dark behind Adeline.

Pushing down the primal need to pounce on the senator and tear him to shreds, Rob's eyes flicked to Adeline's face. It had been years since he'd communicated with another wolf telepathically. Not since his father had sent him running into the woods, to a well-hidden cave when the big trucks with blacked out windows pulled into the town square, blocking off the roads.

Hell, it'd been a long time since he'd run into another of his kind. After getting his "cure", he wouldn't have recognized another wolf if she'd stared him in face. But Adeline? Shouldn't he have known?

Obviously, the cure had only been temporary anyway. Damn!

Follow my lead. Don't give anything away.

What did she know about this situation, about the senator, that he didn't? How was she so calm? Hell, she just winked at him!

"Rob, I'd like you to formally introduce the demon inhabiting Senator Johnson's body." She cocked her head sideways to look up at him.

"Dem...dem...on?" In all his years, Rob knew of their existence but had never met one. Guardian angels...yes. One had helped him find a cure – well, not exactly a cure, but something to suppress his inner beast. Other shifters...not one since his family. Even a vampire once at a club in DC. But a demon?

Ice floated through his veins leaving pinpricks along his arms and the nape of his neck. The calm before the storm.

Rob closed his eyes and concentrated as hard as he could, given there was a gun pressed against Adeline's spine. *Want to fill me in on the plan, sweetheart?*

A soft laugh tickled his brain.

"Well, you gonna leave us in suspense or what? How long you been wearing the bloated, wrinkly meat suit of the senator?"

Rob knew he should've kept his mouth shut, but since when was he one to let a sarcastic comment slide. "Considering the corruption surrounding you, well the senator since his early years in Washington, I'm guessing it's been a long time."

A roar of laughter reverberated through the room. "Why, you are quite right, sir. Johnson hasn't exactly been *here* for some time. Not since we made a little deal the night of the election when it looked like he was going to lose...big. I simply explained that the will of the people could be overridden. Not always. But in his case, I could be of some service. Damn fool didn't even ask the price."

"Nice political science lecture, professor. I bet they don't teach that part in college." Adeline's voice was honeyed, not snippy or even worried for someone who had a gun in their back and their hands bound behind them. Her lips curled up on one side of her mouth. Rob had no clue what her game plan was, but she seemed to be enjoying herself, even with a gun in her back. Quite frankly, it only made her sexier in his eyes.

"Mr. Holden," the senator chuckled, "throw some clothes on, please. You appear to have ripped your own garments, so feel free to take the mangled agent's pants. Then get your ass over to the table with the computer. You have some corrections to make before you die."

Slowly, Rob crouched beside the bloody form of the demon's lackey. Bile rose in his throat. Upon closer inspection, at least it appeared to be a quick kill. Throat was shredded and blood coated most everything, but the rest of the man was intact.

Hands now slick with blood, Rob pulled on the rumpled designer suit pants. Not exactly his size. Vinny's frame had been much smaller than his own. The hem hit him mid-calf and there was no way the zipper was going to close. Looking down at the blood-splattered pants with the fly hanging open for all to see his jewels, Rob almost preferred to remain naked.

Behind him, Adeline snickered, which only made him more self-conscious. Rob prided himself on his body, carefully concealed under the geek attire of ragged t-shirts and khaki pants. To look this ridiculous in front of such an exquisite woman ... ugh!

He walked over to the table. The chair screeched along the metal floor as he pulled it out to sit in front of the archaic computer. "Hey, Senator. You could use an update in your technology. This thing is from the Ice Age."

"Move." The senator's voice was harsh, followed by scuffling sounds as he pushed Adeline across the room.

The senator came to stand immediately behind him. Rob's nose crinkled. That stench! *Do other people in Congress not smell that, or do they all reek of rotten eggs?*

"Now, Mr. Holden, you will put all my money back. Every red cent. Then we'll talk about penance."

"Dude, you can have your filthy blood money, but the world already knows you stole it, killed for it." His fingers pecked away on the keyboard as his mouth ran away with him. He'd been in it for revenge, after tracking down the folks responsible for the death of his friends and family. They'd been in the way of the senator's big vision in cooperation with Nottingham, Inc. Stealing the money back from the senator for those the funds were designated to help in the first place had been incidental, but an added benefit in his estimation. Now the bastard was making him snatch it back. The entire debacle left a bitter taste in mouth...or was that still Vinny's blood coating his tongue?

Keep talking. You're doing great, but don't piss him off too quickly. Give me a chance.

How could Adeline's voice in his head be so calm, as if she were ordering tea instead of plotting an escape from a demonic psychopath? Whatever she was planning, he hoped she'd do it already.

"So, Senator," saccharine sweetness dripped from Adeline's lips, "I'm curious. Seeing as Vinny was my partner for all of two seconds, how long was he your henchman?"

"No, dear. You're asking the wrong question."

"Then, please do enlighten me." Rob caught the reflection of the senator in the monitor as he looked down at Adeline still crouched on the floor. He fought the natural tendency for his lips to curl up in a smile. The woman knew what she was doing...distract AND elicit information.

"You caught my eye about three months ago when you busted the fentanyl ring in Dupont Circle. Your *qualities* were quite evident to even the untrained eye, so I sent my man to discover exactly who and what you are. His findings did not surprise me in the least. Figured I could use someone of your talents, and then this asshat handed you to me on a silver platter, so to speak."

Rob pecked away at the keyboard; all the while Adeline kept the senator talking. The man really was a pompous ass. So self-assured, but Rob guessed most demons were egotistical bastards. He'd wanted to recruit Adeline, so Vinny had placed a tracking device on her bike. They'd sent in the black ops guys, mostly ex-military, from Nottingham's covert division, to extract her for their purposes. Rob didn't even want to think what they wanted her for. Finding him had been merely a *happy accident.*

With the senator barely glancing his way, Rob managed to open up a couple more windows to hide what he was really doing. Any time Johnson looked over, he'd only see a replica of the financial transaction screen. What he wouldn't see would be the messaging system alerting the authorities of a break-in at their location. Also hidden from sight was the code he'd entered to turn on the computer's camera. Everything happening in the room was being fed to an offsite server vault.

"You done yet, hacker boy? I don't have all night."

"Not sure that's incentive for me, considering you are planning on killing us both when I'm finished."

"Oh, you still have some work to do before I gut this pretty young thing with your DNA all over her. Won't be difficult for the police to rule this a sexual assault and murder followed by your own suicide."

Anger coiled within in, like a cocked revolver ready to fire.

Keep it cool. Controlled. Just keep him talking.

Every time her voice sang in his head relief washed over him. Relief and strength. Together they could do this, they could escape and take down the bad guy...together. The word had a nice ring to it. Together. After living and working alone for so long, having a partner to work with felt good.

Hopefully, we don't end up dead and can try this together thing some more.

"Again, my point. Why should I hurry this along? I rather like the living, breathing version of the lady. Not to mention, I like the living and breathing version of myself."

The gun flashed in the computer monitor seconds before it slammed down on his shoulder. The cracking of bone echoed against the steel walls, floor, and ceiling. Pain erupted like a geyser, but quickly faded to a dull ache. "Depending on how quickly you cooperate will determine how much she suffers."

A furious growl erupted behind him as the elderly, but portly man fell into him and they both spilled onto the icy metal floor. The gun banged across the floor and smashed into the wall.

Rob scrambled to regain his balance and threw himself at the senator just as Adeline's lithe body leapt over, her teeth bared. Together they pinned the senator down as her voice rose.

"Exorcizamus te, omnis immundus spiritus, omnis satanica potestas, omnis incursion infernalis adversarii, omnis legio, omnis congregation et secta diabolica."

The more she repeated the words, the harder the demon struggled underneath them. Rob had no idea what she was saying. Adeline leaned down into the senator's face. A cross pendant, dangling from a rope chain around her neck, settled over the man's redden eyes.

With a long hiss, smoke rose from where the jewelry grazed the skin. The body shuttered, rocked, and then slumped back. Rob feared to move. Didn't the villain always spring back to life to kill again? At least, he imagined a demon could very well do that.

Nothing happened. The only sound in the room was their labored breathing and the thrumming of Rob's heart in his chest. Finally, Adeline fell back and lay still, her chest rising and falling in a ragged, irregular rhythm.

"Some first date, huh?" Her laugh filled the dismal room with a lightness he hadn't felt...ever.

"Does this actually qualify for a date? I mean, it's not like we went to dinner and a movie."

Chapter 7

It'd been a week since Adeline had seen Rob Holden. A week since they took down Senator Johnson, or at least the demon that had inhabited the senator for a couple decades. A week since she'd felt her heartbeat inside her chest.

There hadn't been much time to tidy up the crime scene before the police had arrived at the tiny metal vault underneath an abandoned warehouse buried deep in the woods of George Washington National Forest just on the border of West Virginia. Rob had found a pocketknife in Vincent's pants and he used them to cut off her bindings. The wild look in his eyes as he had held her face in his palms and kissed her ... those eyes haunted her.

Adeline knew he would be in the conference room at FBI Headquarters for the debriefing. It was his fate they would be discussing. Apparently, Senator Johnson had powerful friends. Even though the demon was slain, Rob would remain in danger if his identity ever got out. The Attorney General himself had come to her office to detail the roots of corruption that ensnared the senator but went much further, much wider. There were bigger fish to fry. Rob would be the key to bringing down the entire network.

The conversation with the AG left Adeline feeling physically ill and swallowing down the threatening bile. Rob would be in perpetual danger. Despite her skills as a federal agent, and her true identity as a wolf shifter, protecting him would be damn near impossible.

Taking a deep, cleansing breath, Adeline pushed the heavy wooden doors open, expecting to see a room full of suits – agents, marshals, bureaucrats. Her feet rooted to the Persian rug covering the worn Cherrywood planks.

Dusty blonde curls hung over burnt umber eyes staring straight at her as if she were an oasis in the desert. His Adam's apple bobbed as Rob swallowed deeply. No one else was in the room. Even if there had been a hundred people in there, Adeline doubted she'd notice. All she saw, all she could see, was Rob. His lips quirked up on one side, highlighting his dimples.

"Hey, beautiful." His voice was rough as if he hadn't spoken in some time and every syllable broke her heart. They'd been through so much together, but still barely knew each other. Now, their chance had been ripped from them before she'd even recognized it was what she wanted. He would be placed under the witness protection program, and they'd never see each other again. It was better this way. He'd be safe.

Adeline opened her mouth to speak, but a lone strangled sob escaped instead. Rob jumped up from the chair and dashed across the room. Within seconds his strong arms wrapped around her trembling body. Warm, slightly rough hands cradled her face as his lips crushed down on hers, mirroring all the pent-up frustration and fragile emotional state Adeline had experienced over the last few days.

An ember deep within her flared to a roar, sending scorching tendrils through her veins. Until that moment, Adeline had not realized just how cold she'd been. Feverishly, her hands roamed over Rob's chest. Despite the formal business environment, he was still decked out in a worn t-shirt and khaki pants. She felt his heart throbbing against his ribcage through the thin cotton as her fingers splayed across his sculpted pectorals.

"Harrumph." The soft noise sent ice picks through her heart. Adeline instinctively stepped away from Rob, but also moved to stand in front of him in a defensive position. "My apologies for the intrusion, Agent Marion." The agency director towered over them both. At almost seven feet tall. His Dolce & Gabbana navy suit matched his eyes in their intensity, although she caught a twinkle of amusement as he stepped by her with his hand outstretched towards Rob. "Mr. Holden, nice to meet you. It's not every day I get a chance to thank someone for doing my job for me. Taking down Senator Johnson was quite the feat, but I'm afraid it's landed you in a bit of hot water."

Rob's eyebrows furrowed as he evaluated the bureaucrat in front of him. His eyes flicked to hers. With a reassuring nod, she hoped she conveyed that the director was one of the good guys, someone he could trust.

The director settled down in the cushy leather chair at the head of the table before waving his hand for them to join him. "I wanted to meet with you both, together, before letting in the rest of the suits. I hope you don't mind."

"Of course, Director Finlay." Adeline voice found its way back. All business now. Digging her nails into her palms, she re-focused on what was most important ... making sure Rob stayed safe.

"I've read your report, Agent Marion. Quite an entertaining work of fiction." Before she could respond, he raised his hand for quiet. "Don't misunderstand. I get it. You and the hacker took down the sleaziest villain in DC history, at least in this decade. Unorthodox methods, but based on your file, I've come to expect that."

Before the cops arrived to free them from the vault, she had told Rob to follow her lead. Just agree to everything she said. They had been able to make Vinny's death look like the Senator attacked him and Rob had simply fallen on the dead body to account for being covered in the man's blood. The camera on the computer had recorded just enough to indict the senator, but luckily the exorcism was out of the camera's line of sight and the sound quality had been conveniently altered to mute the exorcism chanting. Adeline had crossed her T's and dotted her I's, leaving no potential holes in the story. How did the director know something was not adding up?

A large warm hand came down over her own cradled in her lap. *It's going to be okay. I promise.* Rob's deep voice penetrated through the fog blinding her clarity. With a reassuring squeeze, a calmness fell over her frenzied mind. Adeline raised her gaze to lock with the director's dark eyes.

"Don't jump to conclusions, Agent. Your report has been approved, stamped, and filed away. I'll be the last person to question your methods and I don't care about the specifics. Just the end result. Bad guy outed. Bad guy dead. Case closed. However," his eyes flew to Rob, "that does pose a problem for your cohort in fighting crime."

"Listen, dude …" Only Rob would refer to the top guy at the agency as *dude*. But whatever else he was going to say was drowned out as Director Finlay continued.

"Mr. Holden, as you are now aware, the senator had powerful allies, all entrenched in the same schemes. From what we've been able to uncover, he was actually the low man on the totem pole. And your boss at Nottingham has disappeared completely." He paused, elbows on the large oak table and his index fingers forming a teepee under his chin. "We could use your expertise to take down the entire syndicate."

"Oh, hell no." The words passed her lips before her brain caught up. A tug on her fisted hands held her riveted in the chair.

"I'd be happy to oblige." Adeline's heart plummeted to her toes. So much for keeping Rob safe.

POSSIBLY THE RASHEST decision he'd ever made, but confidence radiated through Rob's body in tiny waves the second the words had left his mouth. Really there had been no decision to make. He had a giant target painted on his back, might was well stand and fight.

Besides, he was exhausted from hiding. He'd hidden his wolf-self, his nature for two decades. Hiding behind his computer screen to track down the men responsible for the slaughter of not just his family, but an entire race of wolf shifters on the east coast. That number had to be in the thousands.

Instead of hiding, what he should've been doing was unleashing the *wolf*, standing to fight for what he wanted.

And he wanted Adeline. Body. Heart. Soul.

Her large almond eyes pierced him, her lips moving in outrage. "What the hell do you think …"

Rob stood, pulled her out of her own chair, and crushed her to his body. "I know what I'm doing. I'm not afraid. But I can only do this with you." A war raged across her features. Confusion. Anger. Perhaps even hope. "Being without you these past few days has been torture. I'll stand and fight by your side any day. No more hiding from the world, from myself."

"I see you two lovebirds have a lot to discuss so I'll leave you be." The director stood to go, but neither Rob nor Adeline paid him any mind. "That is a yes for working with the agency, right? And I believe you'll like your new partner." Rob grunted in reply as the heavy doors swung open and closed behind Director Finlay.

"Rob, are you crazy? Witness protection is what you need. You can't possibly …" He placed two of his fingers over her lips.

"Yes, I am crazy. For you. And I don't need witness protection. All I need is you. Together anything is possible. More than anything, I want to discover all the possibilities of us." Seeing the tears brim in her eyes was like a punch to the gut.

A corner of her mouth ticked up. "Together, huh? You have heard that relationships built on intense experiences don't last."

"Don't know about you, but I love to prove everyone wrong. So, you in?"

Adeline pulled away from him, nearly shattering his resolve. Doubt flooded his veins. Maybe she hadn't felt the same, the vibrant connection, and the fire threading them together. If ever fate reared its head to bite him in the ass, it was this moment.

Unable to breathe, he watched emotions dance across her face as her eyes narrowed on him. Every muscle tensed as a nerve twitched in her clenched jaw. Just as his lungs reached their limit without oxygen, Adeline's face relaxed again. "Oh, hell. Probably going to regret this…"

The rest of her words melted away as she cupped his unshaven chin and pulled him to her. Softly, her lips brushed against his own. Her other hand fisted the curls at the nape of his neck, holding him in place. "Before this gets out of hand, perhaps we should find someplace with a little less traffic."

Taking her hand in his own, they turned and walked out the door, down the stairs and out the back entrance of the J. Edgar Hoover building. For the first time in his life, Rob felt at peace with himself, with the beast that lay dormant within, just under the skin. He could use his gifts for good, and with Adeline by his side, they could do anything.

"So where to, gorgeous?" She pulled him towards a sexy looking beast of metal and fire. A Harley? Yeah, this woman totally rocked his world.

"Just wrap your arms around me and let me take you on the wildest ride of your life."

No need to tell him twice.

THE END

Acknowledgements

HOW WOULD I EVER HAVE published anything without my Scrib Soul Tribe? Thank you lovely ladies for reading, critiquing, rereading, re-critiquing, over and over every word I've ever written.

Special shout out of THANKS to the amazing RA Winter, who not only designed this smoking hot book cover but has been my biggest, more enthusiastic cheerleader along the way. Much love and hugs to you!

Other Books by KC Freeman

Greylyn the Guardian Angel series

BOOK 1 – *Rekindled Prophecy*
   https://books2read.com/u/mq1ZGO
   Book 2 – *Revelations*
   https://books2read.com/u/b5XaWl
   Book 3 – *Redemption*
   https://books2read.com/u/31RXLW
   A boxset with all three ebooks of the series is also available.

Renegade Angel series

BOOK 1 – *Renegade Angel* debuting October 4, 2022 in the
Realm of Darkness boxset
   https://books2read.com/realmofdarknessset[1]

---

1.   https://books2read.com/
realmofdarknessset?fbclid=IwAR2Gb2dBHZMyifSvtw1OWSrtT3oAAplgbt7jFxQw
CEET3QDw82bzASaacLw

Something About Dragons (short story anthology)

HER STORY, ***Dreaming of Dragons***, is a YA Fantasy dragon shifter story which will evolve into its own series.
https://books2read.com/u/3yKa5Z[2]

Falling for the Devil series

CURRENT WORK IN PROGRESS. Estimated release date July/August 2022.

Psychic in Suburbia

CURRENT WORK IN PROGRESS.

Bowman's Inn 2017 Autumn-Winter Anthology

---

2.   https://books2read.com/u/3yKa5Z?fbclid=IwAR0YZPg8PS6-TodAgEdTj9Q1H6468qzQE4Y7727rCbIm0Hl5s46XZceFy2U

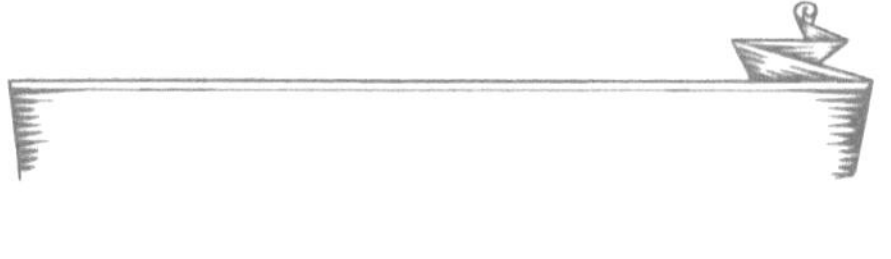

Author Biography

KC Freeman

AFTER LEAVING THE CORPORATE world to raise her five rambunctious children with her husband in North Carolina, KC Freeman eventually found her way back to her lifelong desire to write fiction. First, she dipped her toes in the writing world by ghostwriting cozy mysteries and romance novels before diving headfirst into the fantasy and paranormal romance genres under her own name.

KC writes mostly fantasy and paranormal romance novels. Her preferred subjects are angels and demons as they represent the epic struggles of good versus evil, and she enjoys showcasing how the two ends of the spectrum intermingle for interesting tales and thought-provoking ideas. She also spends a lot of time editing other authors' manuscripts.

When she is not writing, KC is running her children to practices, football games, swim meets, wrestling tournaments, and generally all over town. In her spare time ... who are we kidding? She does not have any of that.

Join KC's newsletter for updates on her new releases, book promos, and book signing events

[HTTP://EEPURL.COM/GDP4JR](http://eepurl.com/gDp4Jr)[1]

---

1. http://eepurl.com/gDp4Jr

Follow the Author

Website

[HTTPS://KCFREEMANAUTHOR.com/](https://kcfreemanauthor.com/)[2]

Facebook

https://www.facebook.com/KCFreemanAuthor

Instagram

[HTTPS://WWW.INSTAGRAM.com/kvcfreeman5/](https://www.instagram.com/kvcfreeman5/)[3]

Twitter

[HTTPS://TWITTER.COM/KCFreeman5](https://twitter.com/KCFreeman5)[4]

---

2. https://kcfreemanauthor.com/

3. https://www.instagram.com/kvcfreeman5/

4. https://twitter.com/KCFreeman5

Who is the hunter and who is the prey?

A clandestine hacker takes from the corrupt political class and gives to their victims. But this time he has gone too far by revealing to the world the absolute evil one politician has wreaked on so many lives.

A sexy FBI agent hunts for The Lone Wolf hacker as her own more primal needs threaten to reveal her true nature and endanger the mission.

Hunted: The Lone Wolf Hunter is a steamy paranormal wolf shifter romance and modern day sexy retelling of the Robin Hood legend.

ISBN 979-8-201-46147-8   201-46147-8